A catalogue record for this book is available from the British Library

Published by Ladybird Books Ltd.
80 Strand, London, WC2R 0RL
A Penguin Company

4 6 8 10 9 7 5 3

The Marrow-Mangler

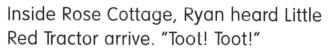

Inside Rose Cottage, Ryan heard Little Red Tractor arrive. "Toot! Toot!"

"Hi Stan! Hello Little Red Tractor!" he called, coming out to meet them.

Stan hopped down from the tractor. He was holding a jar of yucky brown stuff.

"What's that you've got, Stan?" asked Ryan. "It looks horrible!"

Stan explained that the jar was for Amy. "She's not going to drink it!" he laughed. "It's for her marrow."

Amy was in the greenhouse. She was so busy talking to her marrow that she didn't hear Stan and Ryan come in! She'd even given it a name: Maurice.

"I want you to grow even bigger and stronger," she told Maurice. "We're going to win the Best Marrow prize at the fete, aren't we?"

"I've heard that talking to your plants helps them grow," said Stan, handing her the jar. "This'll help even more. It's my special, home-grown plant food. I reckon it'll do your marrow lots of good."

"Thanks, Stan!" Amy was delighted.

Over at Beech Farm, someone else had his eye on the Best Marrow prize. The year before, Stumpy had been the winner. Mr Jones didn't want that to happen again!

"This year we're going to win, aren't we, my beauty?" he told his marrow.

Just then, Mr Jones's nephew Thomas whizzed past on his skateboard.

"Look out!" cried his uncle. "I won't win anything if you skateboard over my marrow!"

"Sorry, Uncle Jasper!" called Thomas. Why on earth was his uncle so bothered about a marrow?

Mr Jones was not the only one. When Stan and Little Red Tractor went over to Stumpy's windmill, Elsie came to the door.

"You won't get any sense out of Stumpy," she said. "He's looking after his marrow."

Just then, Stumpy appeared. He wasn't happy.

"It looks like the birds have got a taste for marrow," he sighed. His marrow had a chunk missing. It wouldn't win now.

"Never mind," said Stan. "We've got some rehearsing to do, remember?" Elsie was puzzled. Whatever did he mean?

Back at Beech Farm, Mr Jones was still worrying about his own marrow when Little Red Tractor pulled up and Stan jumped down.

"Aargh! Careful!" cried Mr Jones. Stan's big boots were too near the marrow for his liking. "There's no way my marrow will beat Stumpy's if you jump on it!" he wailed.

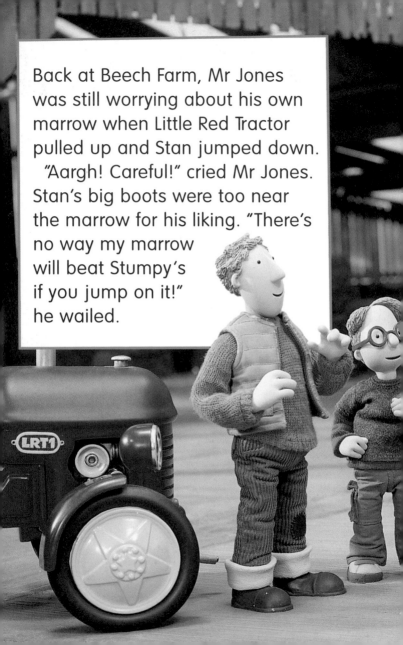

Suddenly, Mr Jones frowned. "What if those birds attack my marrow?" he worried out loud. "Or what if it's not birds at all? There might be a marrow-mangler out there! Thanks for the warning, Stan."

"That's not why I'm here," Stan explained. "I came to remind you about the rehearsal."

"What rehearsal?" Thomas wanted to know. But Stan put his finger to his lips.

"It's a secret," he grinned.

Little Red Tractor looked excited. He was in on the secret, too!

Stan's next stop was the garage.
"Is Walter about?" he asked Nicola.
Suddenly...**BOOM!**
  An explosion behind the garage
showed someone was at work!
Stan grinned at Nicola. He knew
who was to blame!
  Nicola looked puzzled. "What was
that?" she asked.

"Hi there, Stan! Hello, Little Red Tractor!" called Walter. He was covered in soot!

"I just popped round to see how you're sorted for a spot of rehearsing," said Stan.

Nicola was curious. "Rehearsing?" she asked.

"You'll see ... so long as you come to the fete," laughed Stan.

That night, Mr Jones took one last look at his precious marrow. A horrible thought struck him.

"What if there's a marrow-mangler on the loose?" he muttered. It was no good, he just couldn't risk leaving the marrow on its own. With a deckchair, some cheese sandwiches and a flask of tea, he settled down to watch over it. But as the moon rose in the sky, Mr Jones's eyes began to close…

Even in his sleep, Mr Jones had marrows on his mind. Muttering about the marrow-mangler, he began to sleepwalk. Perhaps he shouldn't have eaten those cheese sandwiches!

Clomp! Clomp! The sleepwalking farmer clomped right across the marrow. His size nines did terrible damage. Then he flopped down in his chair again, leaving one shoe behind.

Morning came at last. Mr Jones opened his eyes and had just one thing to say: **"Aaaaaarghhhh!"**

Mr Jones got straight on the phone to Stan. He needed help to track down the marrow-mangler!

"I'll be right there!" said Stan. "Come on, Little Red Tractor."

Stan soon realised that the only marrow-mangler at Beech Farm was Mr Jones himself.

"See those footprints? And that trail of sandwich crumbs … and your shoe?" Stan couldn't help grinning.

"You mean ... it was me?"
Mr Jones was as crushed as
his marrow.

"Cheer up," said Stan. "We've
still got a surprise for everyone!"

That afternoon, the whole of Babblebrook seemed to be at the fete. But where were Stan, Walter, Stumpy and Mr Jones?

"Ladies and gentlemen, boys and girls!" the announcer rang out. "Prepare to be thrilled and amazed by the daredevil skills of the Babblebrook Display Team!"

Roaring into the arena came
Mr Jones and his tractor Big Blue,
Stumpy and his quad bike Nipper,
Walter and his pick-up truck
Sparky, and, of course, Stan and
Little Red Tractor.

Wow! The audience gasped at
their brilliant display.

After the applause, even Mr Jones was smiling.

"That almost made up for not winning the Best Marrow prize," he told Stan. "Did you hear who won it, by any chance?"

"Me and Maurice!" called Amy, proudly showing her rosette.

"Well done!" smiled Mr Jones. "But you'll have me to beat next year!"

Ryan had a question for Stan. "Are you and Little Red Tractor doing another show next year?"

"Toot! Toot!" Little Red Tractor had something to say!

"That sounds like a 'yes' to me!" laughed Stan.